Friday
the Scaredy Cat

The Scariest Day Ever ... So Far

Kara McMahon ✦ illustrated by Maddy McClellan

Ready-to-Read

Simon Spotlight

New York London Toronto Sydney New Delhi

SIMON SPOTLIGHT

An imprint of Simon & Schuster Children's Publishing Division

1230 Avenue of the Americas, New York, New York 10020

Copyright © 2013 Simon & Schuster, Inc.

SIMON SPOTLIGHT, READY-TO-READ, and colophon are registered trademarks of Simon & Schuster, Inc.

For information about special discounts for bulk purchases, please contact Simon & Schuster Special Sales at 1-866-506-1949 or business@simonandschuster.com.

The Simon & Schuster Speakers Bureau can bring authors to your live event. For more information or to book an event contact the Simon & Schuster Speakers Bureau at 1-866-248-3049 or visit our website at www.simonspeakers.com.

Manufactured in the United States of America 0713 LAK

First Edition

10 9 8 7 6 5 4 3 2 1

Library of Congress Cataloging-in-Publication Data

McMahon, Kara.

The scariest day ever — so far / by Kara McMahon ; [illustrated by Maddy McClellan]. — First edition.

pages cm. — (Friday the scaredy cat) (Ready-to-read)

Summary: "There are new things in Friday's house: a new bed, a new bowl, a new toy mouse. There are new smells and new noises, too. Friday is scared. What do these things mean? Is it a monster… could it be a new little sister?" — Provided by publisher.

ISBN 978-1-4424-6694-4 (hardback) —

ISBN 978-1-4424-6693-7 (trade paper) —

ISBN 978-1-4424-6695-1 (ebook)

[1. Cats—Fiction. 2. Fear—Fiction.] I. McClellan, Maddy, illustrator. II. Title.

PZ7.M478752Sc 2013

[E]—dc23

2012051447

This is Friday the Scaredy Cat.
Today was the scariest day
of his life.
Here is what happened:

This morning Friday woke up
and saw a new pink bed
next to his blue bed.

It was different, so he
was scared.
Friday hid under the rug.

A few hours later
Friday came out.
He crept past the new bed
and saw a new pink bowl
next to his blue bowl!

It was different, so he
was scared.
Friday hid behind the sofa.

A few hours later
Friday came out again.
He crept past the new bed
and the new bowl
and saw a pink toy mouse.

It was different, so he
was scared.
Friday hid under the blanket.

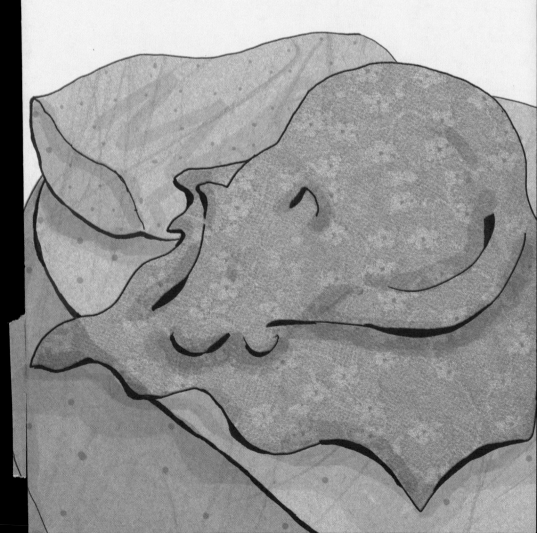

A few hours later
Friday came out again.
He did not see anything new.
But then he smelled
something new!

Friday hid behind
the curtains.

A few hours later
Friday came out again.
He did not smell anything new.
But then he heard
something new!

Meow!
Meow!

Friday hid behind
the plant.

A few hours later
Friday came out again.
A white blur flashed
in front of him.
It was a monster!

Friday hid in the closet.

The monster followed Friday.
"I have been waiting
to meet you all day!"
said the monster.

"You will be scared of me!"
said Friday.
"I am not scared of
anything!" said the monster.

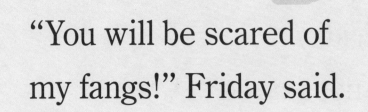
"You will be scared of
my fangs!" Friday said.

"I am not scared of
anything!" said the monster.
"And look! I have fangs too!"

So, very slowly, Friday came
out of the closet to meet . . .

his new sister!
She is a tiny cat!
She is not a monster!
Her name is Angela.

Friday is excited.
He has a new sister!

She is not a monster!
She is not scared of
anything!

Today started out scary
but turned out great!
Maybe this was not the
scariest day ever.
There is always tomorrow.